The *Adventures of Mortimer* Trilogy

BOOK II

A Kingdom Divided

Kevin J. Kurtz

The Books in the *The Adventures of Mortimer* Trilogy

BOOK ONE

Mortimer and the Powerful Sword

BOOK TWO

A Kingdom Divided

BOOK THREE

The King Revealed

Acknowledgements

To Wendy, my wife, who is my biggest inspiration, and my #1 fan. She's the first reader of my rough drafts. Her insights lead to a finished manuscript that I can be proud of.

I also want to give credit to Sue Clark, who has helped ignite in me a passion for writing, and the encouragement to not fear the editing process.

I cannot fail to mention all of the readers of Book I who contacted me with glowing comments regarding Mortimer and the Powerful Sword. You have all motivated me to finish the trilogy in a timely manner. May you continue to be inspired by the Adventures of Mortimer.

CONTENTS

The Queen's Business

Mortimer's glee at the thought of returning to Queen Valora faded. A dread, a sense of gloom crossed through his mind. Gwendolyn had left him at the cliff's edge. Eonder abandoned him on the North Road. His mother sailed the sea with a man who flattered her.

Mortimer was alone. An ache gripped his heart, and spread to his bones. He slumped forward on his horse.

"Come on, boy. Quit your lagging. Or we'll leave you for the Kardoc's beak."

The three castle guards laughed at Langwyn's joke.

Mortimer nudged his mare to quicken her pace. Pockets of fog hung close to the ground, blocking out the morning sun. Mortimer shivered.

The stench of sulfur and putrefying flesh shocked Mortimer. A huge black bird appeared through the fog with its wings stretched wide and its talons spread forward. The giant bird shrieked as it snatched one of the castle guards off his horse and lifted him into the air. Mortimer looked up to see the guard flailing his arms as he hung down in the grip of the giant bird's talons. His helmet flew off and fell to the earth, clanging on the shalestone rock at Mortimer's feet.

"The Kardoc got Col," one guard screamed.

The other two guards had already bolted their horses toward the castle.

"Stay together," Langwyn, the lead guard shouted, "or you'll feel the tip of my blade."

The two guards slowed their stallions.

"Look lively. We're nearing the gate," Langwyn said.

"What if the Black Bird comes back? It killed Col."

"Quit your sniveling and keep your eyes open. When we get to the Castle, I'll do the talking." Langwyn slowed his stead to a trot.

The sun burned away the last inland wisps of fog. Mortimer watched the sun's rays reflect off the glistening towers as they approached the White Castle. A sentry, holding a long lance, stepped forward from the castle gate. "Halt! State your purpose."

Langwyn stopped. "Returning from the Queen's business," he said.

Out of the corner of his eye, Mortimer saw a bird spread its wings and drop down into a glide from a tall tree. It let out a "scree" sound as it approached the guards on their horses.

"It's the Black Bird of Death," one guard screamed as he jumped off his horse and lay on the ground, trying to hide. The small bird swooped down low, right over Mortimer's head, then perched on the western tower of the White Castle.

"What's this all about?" the sentry said.

"Never mind him. He's just jumpy. Thought he saw a Kardoc. You know, Black Bird of Death?" Langwyn got off of his horse and slapped the top of the guard's helmet as he lay on the ground. "Get up, you dolt. It was just a hawk."

"Actually, I think it was a falcon," the sentry spoke up.

Mortimer covered his mouth and snickered.

Langwyn glared at Mortimer. "Are you going to open the gate, or what?" he snapped at the sentry.

"Right away, sir. Go about your business." The sentry signaled and the iron gate opened.

Once the guards returned the horses to the stable, Langwyn grabbed hold of Mortimer's arm. "So you're a smart kid, eh?" Langwyn turned to the two guards. "You go back to your stations. And not a word about Col. I'll talk to the Queen." Still holding Mortimer's arm, Langwyn walked across the courtyard and up the steps to the wooden arched door of Queen Valora's inner court. He knocked.

"Enter," a woman's voice said.

Langwyn opened the door and stepped into the room. Ghimel, Queen Valora's Advisor, stood next to her as she sat on her throne, holding her golden scepter in her lap. Her raven-black hair hung straight down over her shoulders.

"Step forward. Do you have something to report?" the Queen said.

"Yes, your Ladyship, from our morning ride." Langwyn held tight to Mortimer's arm, as Mortimer wiggled to break free.

"Is there a reason why you are holding the boy's arm?" The Queen used a sharp tone.

"Uh...no, ma'am...your Ladyship." Langwyn loosened his grip. Mortimer pulled away and rubbed his arm where Langwyn had pressed his fingers into Mortimer's skin.

"You are testing my patience. Tell me what happened."

"Yes, yes, your Ladyship. I took the boy and the girl riding, as you instructed." Langwyn patted Mortimer on the head. "It was a lovely ride. Down the coastal path."

"Go on."

"Yes, we were riding, as you instructed, and, well, a giant, black bird attacked us."

"A giant bird, you say?"

"Yes, your Ladyship, a Kardoc, a Black Bird of Death, swooped down upon us. Me and my men fought it off with our swords, brave lads. We formed a circle to protect the children. The Black Bird circled back and took one of the men. Lifted him right into the sky."

"And what of the girl?"

"The girl?"

Queen Valora leaned forward and glared at Langwyn. "The girl that was riding with you. What happened to her?"

Langwyn began to perspire. "She was carried off when me and my men were knocked to the ground."

"So, the bird, as you say, carried off one of your men and the girl?"

Langwyn lowered his eyes.

Queen Valora looked at Mortimer. "Is this true?"

Mortimer looked at Langwyn. He thought about how the guards hid from the Black Bird of Death in the bushes, and how Gwendolyn and her horse were standing just below the cliff's edge. He remembered Gwendolyn telling him to take care of himself, that she was going to find her grandfather.

Mortimer pictured Eonder in his mind, riding off and leaving Gwendolyn and him alone. It was Eonder's fault that all of this happened. Mortimer bit his lip. "Yes, it is true."

"How tragic. You poor dear. Come here." Queen Valora let the scepter rest in her lap as she opened her arms. Mortimer walked toward her, head bent. He smelled lilac as the Queen hugged him close.

Ghimel raised an eyebrow and lifted his long, crooked nose in the air.

Queen Valora pushed Mortimer's hair to the side and kissed him on the forehead. "Take a hot bath, then come for supper. I am sure you will feel better after you have had something to eat." The Queen looked at Langwyn. "Escort him to his room."

Langwyn bowed toward the Queen and Ghimel, then walked with Mortimer out the door and down the hall. "That could have been a cooker, eh, if she had caught us in a fancy tale?" Langwyn said.

Mortimer rubbed his arm again and scowled before slamming his bedroom door shut in the guard's face.

The Queen's Plan

CHAPTER 2

Mortimer plopped on his bed. He smelled the sea breeze in the wind that blew in through his open window. "Gwendolyn, where are you?" He buried his face in a pillow.

Baldor, his servant, had already picked an outfit for him to wear and laid it out on the bed. Mortimer wiped his eyes. "At least here I am appreciated."

Mortimer unstrapped his golden helmet and laid it near the pillows. "I will dress like a prince." Mortimer huffed. "And someday I will marry the Queen." He pulled out his pointy stick from the belt loop his mother had sewn, and waved it in the air. "I am Mortimer, the Prince of the White Castle." Mortimer slipped out of his clothes and into the steamy bath Baldor had prepared.

Later, he picked up the navy velvet shirt that poofed at the shoulders and felt the fine quality of the fabric.

Mortimer put on the shirt and matching navy britches, and was just about to put on a navy velvet hat that looked like a crossed bun, when a falcon flew in the window and perched on the ledge.

Mortimer jumped back. The bird blinked its eyes and cocked its head.

The knock on the door startled Mortimer. "Come in."

Baldor entered the room.

"Baldor, look at the bird in my window."

"Well, Master Mortimer, it seems you have acquired a friend."

"A friend? This bird looks more fierce. I mean, look how sharp its beak and talons are."

"Young squire, I am but a page. But I believe this is a falcon, a bird of prey."

"What do they do?"

"Men of nobility train them to catch small game."

"Do you think I could do it?" Mortimer stepped with his hand outstretched and the falcon flew away.

"I am sorry. Maybe it will return," Baldor said.

Mortimer folded his arms and pursed his lips.

"No time to sulk, sire. The Queen has summoned you."

Mortimer placed the navy velvet hat on his head and smiled. "How do I look?"

"Like a prince."

"Good. Then I am off to see the Queen."

Mortimer walked down the hall from his room. Torches hung from the stone walls, lighting the way. Mortimer stood outside the banquet room door and adjusted his velvet cap. He took a deep breath and knocked.

"Come in," the Queen said.

When Mortimer stepped through the door, he saw Queen Valora at the far end of the banquet table. Ghimel sat to her left.

"Come in, young one. Come sit by me." The Queen motioned to the vacant seat to her right.

Mortimer hurried to the open chair. He stared at her long, black hair and her beautiful green eyes.

Queen Valora snapped her fingers. An attendant poured from a flagon into Mortimer's silver goblet. "Drink this. It will make you feel better," she said.

Mortimer lifted his head and took hold of the goblet. The dark liquid looked shiny inside as he swirled it around. It warmed his throat all the way down to his belly.

"Would you like to talk about your day?" the Queen said.

Mortimer thought about riding off and leaving Gwendolyn his friend at the cliff. He closed his eyes and shook his head no.

Queen Valora snapped her fingers. The attendants placed several silver platters on the table and then with ceremony, they lifted the lids of each to reveal honey-glazed ham, pork chops in marmalade, bread pudding with plum sauce, blackberry tarts, and brittle toffee.

There were no vegetables.

"Do you approve, young one?"

"Yes, everything looks fine." Mortimer remembered his first meal with the Queen. He had been so hungry, and the food had looked so good, yet when he chewed it the food had no flavor. His stomach felt empty when he finished.

He stabbed a piece of ham, bit and swallowed. "Mmm, that is good." He took a long drink to wash it down.

The Queen watched and smiled.

Mortimer filled his plate, then when he finished, he leaned back in his chair and burped. "Excuse me," he said.

Queen Valora laughed. "What a delightful boy. I am glad the meal helped you forget your troubles." She snapped her fingers and the attendant filled Mortimer's goblet. "Tell me more about your ride this morning."

Mortimer took a drink to wet his throat. "We rode the horses down the coast...and then a Kardoc attacked us." He looked at the Queen for her reaction, but he saw none. "The Kardoc took Gwendolyn away." He lowered his eyes.

"There, there, you poor dear. What a dreadful thing for you to see your friend carried off like that. You must have been terrified." The Queen reached over and patted Mortimer's hand.

"No. I mean, I had seen the Kardoc before."

"Yes, that is right...on your other adventures. Tell me, did you fight it off with your sword?"

Mortimer took a gulp from the goblet and felt his head get woozy. He imagined his pointy stick glowing blue as he pulled it from his belt loop to slash at the giant Black Bird swooping down upon them. "Yes, I did. I think I wounded it."

Ghimel snorted.

"My, my, you are an exceptionally brave boy. Most men would quake with fear at the sight of a Kardoc."

Mortimer puffed out his chest.

Queen Valora turned toward Ghimel. "Ghimel, leave us for a moment."

Ghimel's eyes widened. "My Queen, I have never left your side."

"Oh, Ghimel, stop acting like a child. There is merely something I want to say to the boy...in private."

Ghimel flashed an angry glare at Mortimer before pushing his chair from the table and stomping out the rear door.

"Now, where were we?" the Queen said. "Oh, yes. We were discussing what a special young man you are."

Mortimer felt his face get hot.

The Queen leaned closer. "Do you think you could do something special for me?"

"Yes. Whatever you want."

"That is good, because I will need someone very brave and someone I can trust."

"I am brave. You can trust me."

Queen Valora picked up her scepter. "I have my scepter, but a thief stole my crown. Some days I do not feel like a queen without my crown." The Queen narrowed her eyes. "I believe you know where it is."

"What? I did not take it."

The Queen laughed. "Of course you did not take it. But you have seen it. It is made of polished gold and is set with diamonds, emeralds and pearls."

Mortimer's head felt a little fuzzy, but he tried to picture what the Queen was describing. "I have seen it. In Gharma's cave. Sitting on the top of a pile of gold."

"Do you remember how to get there?"

Mortimer was starting to get a headache. "I think so."

"Good. Here is my plan. I would like you to go with Ghimel and some of my troops. Show them the way to Gharma's cave and bring back the crown to me."

Mortimer rubbed his stomach. He felt sick. "When do you want us to go?"

"You can get an early start in the morning." Queen Valora squeezed Mortimer, then kissed him on the forehead. Mortimer smelled the lilac in her hair and on her neck. He felt her heart beat as his face pressed against her chest.

"And Mortimer," the Queen said, "I reward those who please me."

That was the last thing Mortimer remembered before the room started spinning and his eyes closed.

Gwendolyn's Rescue

CHAPTER 3

Gwendolyn held the reins of her horse as they walked together along the ledge. She stood on her toes to peer over the sagebrush at the edge of the cliff to see if Mortimer was still there. He had gone, and so had the soldiers.

She took several more steps then slipped on the loose stone, cutting her hands as she reached down to brace her fall. Her dress snagged on a gnarled bristlecone pine branch.

She looked down the cliff and felt dizzy, her foot pushed pebbles far, far below into the white-tipped waves. The horse snorted. "Sorry to scare you, girl," she said to the mare. Gwendolyn noticed the blood on her scraped palms and the tear in her pale blue dress. "What a shame. I was growing fond of this dress." She brushed off the dust. "I will be more careful."

The mare nodded her head.

"Lord, please help me. I need to find my grandfather," she said. Gwendolyn thought back to the road to Hamendal.

Her grandfather left her and Mortimer with instructions to find King William's friend, the Caretaker, at the White Castle. They had found that friend, locked in the tower by the Queen's order.

Mortimer did not believe her, would not even listen when she tried to tell him there was something wrong with Queen Valora.

That left her no choice. She would have to go alone.

"We need to go down the cliff, girl."

The mare neighed.

"No, we cannot go back. Not to the White Castle. And if the soldiers do not find us, the Black Bird will."

The horse stomped her foot.

"I know. I am afraid, too. We will go slow, with God's help."

Gwendolyn picked up the reins and inched her way downward in a zigzag pattern with her back to the cliff. She leaned her weight against the sandstone cliff, holding out her left hand to feel for the wall. In spite of the cold mist rising up from the crashing waves below, perspiration beaded up on her forehead and rolled down her face.

By midday, Gwendolyn reached a point where the ledge ahead split into narrow shards that plunged down to the water. The rock there was wet from the pounding ocean. Gwendolyn took a deep breath and lowered herself onto the rock, feeling for a foothold. "Be careful, girl, it is slippery," she said as she guided her horse onto the rock.

Gwendolyn's stomach groaned and her head ached, and she was so thirsty. The sun had dropped lower into the sky and now beat on top of her head. It had been hours since she had a nibble of bread at breakfast. It was Queen Valora's fault that she skipped her meal.

She huffed. "I am going to climb down these rocks and find my grandfather. He will tell King William about that wicked woman and that will be the end of her."

More than once Gwendolyn felt the mare's footing slip on the jagged rock. Gwendolyn reached up to steady her horse, and to keep her from falling into the waves smashing below. They continued to inch their way downward.

The waves had receded with the low tide, revealing a sandy beach below. Gwendolyn could see a way down to the beach that was not as steep. "Just a little farther, girl," she said.

Another hour passed before her foot touched the sand. When her horse had all four hooves on the ground, Gwendolyn hugged her neck. "We made it, girl. You were very brave." She kissed her horse on her nose, feeling the mare's sweat. "Can you ride, girl? I must find my grandfather." The mare neighed.

Gwendolyn looked up at the precipice she had conquered that day. She could see no pathway along the sheer wall of the cliff. How had she had been able to get down to the beach?

"Thank you, Lord, for bringing me safely down the rocks." Gwendolyn squeezed her eyes shut. "And please watch over Mortimer."

She grabbed the reins and hopped onto the saddle. They moved south along the beach as the sun dropped low on the horizon. Just as she began to wonder what she would do when it got dark, Gwendolyn saw a figure up ahead.

As she got closer she could see an old man mending a fishing net. The net hung over a line between two stick poles stuck in the sand. The old man sat on a wooden stool, running a needle through the net, cinching the thread tight with his teeth.

The hairs on top of his head, as well as his beard, were as white as snow. His tanned face and hands were leathery from years of sun and saltwater.

"Excuse me," Gwendolyn said.

"Blessed be!" The old man jumped off his stool. "You scared the wits out of me. What's the idea of sneaking up on ol' Ben like that?"

"I am sorry, I did not mean to scare you."

"Well, you gave me a start, you did." Ben looked down the beach from where Gwendolyn had come. "Say, how'd you get here?"

Gwendolyn got off her horse. Her knees buckled and she fell forward. Ben reached out to catch her, guiding her down upon the stool.

"Rest here. I'll get some water." Ben went up to a wooden shack set back against the cliffs. A small rowboat leaned against the side of the shack. He returned with a tin cup. "Here, drink this."

Gwendolyn took a sip. The water felt cool going down her parched throat. "Thank you," She handed the cup back.

Ben pushed the cup back into her hand. "Lass, you need to drink it all." He seemed to notice the cuts on her palms and the blood on her knees.

Gwendolyn emptied the tin. "Thank you, again, I feel much better."

"Are you feeling well enough to tell me how you got here?"

Gwendolyn thought about the Queen and the soldiers and her ride with Mortimer that morning. "Well, I was out riding from the White Castle. I got too close to the edge and I fell over, onto a ledge." She stopped to look at the old fisherman.

Ben stroked his white whiskers. "Go on."

"I could not get back over the ledge, so I decided to come down."

Ben waited for Gwendolyn to say more. "So you're saying that you, and your horse, came down the cliff near the White Castle?"

Gwendolyn nodded. "Yes, I am."

Ben stroked his beard, then threw up his arms. "Blessed be, girl. I've heard some tales in my day, but that's the strangest story I've ever heard or my name isn't Bendarwyn Pendragon. A girl, and her horse, climbing down a cliff, showing up at my door like a ghost."

"I am sorry I scared you. I was trying to get to my grandfather."

Ben sat on the sand next to Gwendolyn. "Got a granddaughter of my own. Don't worry, lass, I'll help you." Ben looked back at his tiny shack. "I won't be able to help you here, though. I'll get you to the city."

Ben helped Gwendolyn onto her horse and guided the two of them over craggy rocks that jutted out from the cliff, and through a tunnel formed by years of pounding surf. The tunnel opened onto smooth sand. At high tide this route would be covered in foaming water. Ben then led them up a path overgrown by bushes. After he wove his way around and through the bushes, he stopped on a knoll and pointed his finger. "There is the city of Helgath."

Gwendolyn and The Lion's Paw

CHAPTER 4

Gwendolyn sat on her horse as Ben led them down the sandy knoll and onto a cobblestone road. Ahead she saw a stone tower and an open gate. A sentry stood at attention as a column of soldiers filed out of the city.

The column marched in pairs along the cobblestone road. Ben nudged Gwendolyn and her horse off the road and out of the way of the soldiers.

Once the soldiers had passed, Ben and Gwendolyn continued toward the city.

"Halt, state your business," the sentry stuck out his hand.

Ben stopped with a lurch. "No business. Just here to visit a friend."

The sentry smirked. "Well, I don't think an old man and a girl pose a threat to Helgath. You can pass." He lowered his hand.

Ben guided them through an entry stone tunnel into an open courtyard. Gwendolyn smelled fish before she heard the vendor shout, "Fresh halibut and flounder." Another vendor shouted louder, "A chicken for your pot or chicken pot pie."

A squad of soldiers entered the courtyard and began to push the people aside. A crier rang a bell, "Make way for Lord Llandon."

Lord Llandon rode a white horse in the center of the squad of soldiers. He wore a blue velvet jacket with black fur trim at the collar. On his head sat a blue velvet cap with a peacock feather on the side. Lord Llandon did not acknowledge the crowd around him.

Some people did not move fast enough at the crier's orders. The soldiers lowered their pole-axes, jabbing at those who were closest. Someone screamed, which set off the crowd scurrying in every direction.

Gwendolyn's mare was pushed against a vendor's table. When the horse raised her front legs, Gwendolyn fell off onto the cobblestone. Ben held the horse's reigns to keep the mare from bolting.

A man and a woman standing nearby forced their way through the crowd to get to Gwendolyn. The man reached down with one arm to pick her up while shoving people aside with the other.

"Are you alright?" the woman said.

The man placed Gwendolyn on her feet. She looked down at her hands and knees. Red started to ooze through the bandages Ben had put on. "I seem to have opened my wounds."

"What kind of people would do that?" the woman said.

"The kind that are stirred by those wild animals." The man raised his voice and turned toward the soldiers as he spoke, but the squad and Lord Llandon had already passed out of earshot.

"Those wounds will need to be tended to." The woman touched Gwendolyn on the shoulder.

"I was taking her to The Lion's Paw," Ben said.

"How strange. That is where we are headed. The proprietor is a friend of mine." The man placed Gwendolyn on her horse. "Shall we go together? My name is Oberon."

"And mine is Marallon."

Gwendolyn looked at the man built like a bear. His green eyes showed compassion and tenderness. The golden lion crest on his left breast pocket signified service to King William. The woman wore a modest dress. Her hazel eyes showed an inner strength and beauty.

"Yes, we should go together," Gwendolyn said.

The four made their way through the booths where vendors were picking up their overturned tables and carts. They were careful to step over the spilled vegetables and fruit as they passed by. The courtyard narrowed to a single lane, then split to the left and to the right.

Oberon looked down the lane to the left. "I will have to pay those soldiers a visit."

Marallon tugged on his arm and frowned.

"But not tonight," Oberon said as he steered toward the right. "Tonight we eat roast mutton with friends. Here we are at The Lion's Paw." Oberon reached up and straightened the drooping sign, reattaching it to the hook.

A door opened across the lane. A man with his arm around a woman stumbled out into the street and passed down an alley into darkness.

Oberon pulled open the door of The Lion's Paw and stepped in. "Angwin," Oberon's voice boomed.

A short, round man appeared from a side room. "Well, now you have gone and done it. Raised the dead and scared my chickens."

Oberon laughed. "I have brought friends to dine on your famous mutton." He motioned for the others to enter.

Angwin stepped forward to greet his guests as Gwendolyn got off her horse. Before she could ask, Angwin said, "I will see that your mare is fed oats and groomed."

Gwendolyn hugged her horse's neck and kissed her on the nose before she entered The Lion's Paw Inn. Angwin extended his hand, then noticed the blood on Gwendolyn's bandages.

"Oh, my." Angwin turned around and yelled in the direction of the room he came from. "Mother, there is a child here who needs your doctoring."

A short, plump woman came into the room, wiping her hands on her apron. "Now, what is all the fuss about?" She walked to Gwendolyn, saw her hands and knees, and said, "Poor dear. Come with me and I will fix you right up."

Oberon pinned Angwin's arms to his side with a big hug, dwarfing the smaller man. "Have you missed me?"

Angwin caught his breath. "Yes, like the bees miss the black bear who steals their honey."

Oberon laughed. "It is a delightful coincidence to see you again after all these years, and not more than three days after Eonder's visit."

Gwendolyn screamed. "Eonder is my grandfather! I am looking for him, I mean, I am not lost...we were traveling together and then I went to the White Castle and she was there and I knew she was bad so I escaped and came down the cliff."

"Slow down. Take a breath," Oberon said. "We will hear all about your story over dinner, and after your wounds are cleaned."

Marallon spoke up. "Did you happen to see a young boy with your grandfather?"

"Do you mean Mortimer? Oh yes, we are quite good friends. At least I think so...until the witch in the castle..."

All the adults said, "Witch?" at the same time.

"Well, I do not know if she is really a witch, I mean..."

Oberon scratched his black beard while Marallon gave him a worried glance. "Young one, we have much to talk about. But first get your wounds tended to." Gwendolyn left the room with Angwin's wife. "Angwin, my friend, I am afraid there will not be much laughter tonight."

"I am grateful for your company. I will have your dinners ready shortly."

Oberon, Marallon and Ben sat down at a table. "The child said some things that vex me. She mentioned a witch in the White Castle."

"What do you think it means?" Marallon said.

"I don't know about the castle," Ben spoke up, "but there's some strange happenings here in Helgath."

Oberon stroked his beard and started to speak, then stopped when he saw Gwendolyn and Angwin's wife emerge from the side room. Angwin reappeared from the kitchen holding steaming platters.

Angwin placed trenchers of roast mutton, filet of fish, bread and butter, and blackberry tarts on the table.

"Angwin, you bring a smile to my belly," Oberon said.

Marallon asked Gwendolyn how she met Mortimer and that got her started. She went on about Eonder and Mortimer coming to her cabin and their journey in the Narrow Woods and Eonder leaving them at the Hamendal road that traveled north, and then the discovery of the garden.

Gwendolyn stopped when she realized everyone was looking at her in an odd way. She blushed. "I am sorry, I have prattled on."

Oberon chuckled, "We were wondering when you were going to come up for air."

Over the course of the meal Gwendolyn was able to tell how they met Queen Valora and the Caretaker in the tower. "The Queen was nice at dinner. Mortimer was gushing over her. It made me ill. I knew something was not right and that I had to find my grandfather. We went riding in the morning and I saw my chance to escape when the Kardoc attacked. Well, I made my way down the cliff, my horse and I, and I saw Ben."

Ben scratched his head. "I never heard of no one coming down that cliff."

Angwin came to collect the plates. "I have rooms to spare for all of you. You can get a good night's rest. Mother, come show the young lady to her room."

Gwendolyn left with Angwin's wife. The thought of a soft bed and sleep overcame her.

Angwin sat down. He leaned in. "There is more to tell, but the girl need not hear."

As Angwin opened his mouth to speak, the front door creaked open. A man's figure in a dark green cloak stood in the doorway. The hood of the cloak covered his face.

Angwin, Ben, Oberon, and Marallon turned toward the uninvited guest.

Warrant For Their Arrest

CHAPTER 5

The figure stood in the doorway for a second, leaning on his walking stick before throwing back his hood. "Is this a private party, or are old friends invited, too?"

Oberon stood up. "My Lord," he said as he bowed.

Eonder approached the table where the others were sitting and sat next to Angwin. "May I join you, friend?"

"By all means. You are always welcome at my establishment, my Lord," Angwin said. "Have you eaten yet? I am sure I could prepare something."

"Thank you, Angwin. I have had my supper. I am curious, though, to hear what you were discussing."

"Well, then, where was I? I was about to tell about Llandon...and mother put your granddaughter to bed. By the Lord above, I forgot to tell you, Gwendolyn is here."

"I trust she is sleeping in one of your comfortable beds?"

"Yes, of course, and well fed, too. Quite a day she has had. Poor thing is exhausted." Oberon cleared his throat. "Yes, well, I am sure she would want to tell you the details in the morning."

"You were talking of Llandon," Eonder said.

"Yes, I was. About six months ago Llandon rode into town with an armed escort. Two days later the nobles called a town meeting in the square to announce that Lord Llandon was now steward of Helgath and that he would prepare the garrison for the king's arrival. That is about the time the extra soldiers arrived."

"I remember the night the soldiers came ashore." Ben said. "I was mending my nets by the light of the moon when I saw three boats row up to the dock. I could hear their armor clang as they got out. There was a larger ship anchored off shore. Didn't recognize its flag."

Angwin spoke up. "Yes, well I have seen some of those new soldiers in town. They have been regulars at that place," he pointed to the inn across the street. "Bullies, ruffians, drunkards. Cleg the Miller and Bryn the Smithy went to Llandon to complain. They have not been seen since."

Eonder stroked his long beard. "Perhaps it is time to pay Llandon a visit. Oberon, would you care to join me?"

Oberon cracked his knuckles. "I would, sire. Maybe we can teach them some manners?"

Eonder touched Oberon on the shoulder. "Thank you, friend. We will get an early start after a night's rest."

"I have prepared rooms for all of you. It is my honor to have you at my establishment," Angwin said.

Marallon approached Eonder as he stood up and curtsied. "Beg your pardon, my lord, but do you have word of my boy? Gwendolyn has brought news that troubles me."

Eonder put his hand on her shoulder. "It is true that Mortimer has felt the enticement of Valora. But rest assured, my lady, the King has eyes in many places. I will not forget the promise I made to thee."

Eonder and Oberon were up before the others. They talked in hushed tones as they finished their breakfast.

"I have known Llandon a long time," Eonder said, "It is not like him to make so bold a move."

"Well, he acted quite bold, smug even, as he rode through the square yesterday," Oberon said.

"Yes, I believe he was confident with the soldiers there to prop him up. Someone certainly was behind his new appointment, and I can assure you it was not the king. It is time for our visit." Eonder left a parchment addressed to Gwendolyn on the table.

The two men stepped out of The Lion's Paw onto the cobblestone road. Across the street, a man slumped in the doorway of The Spider's Lair, a bottle of wine in his lap. Eonder and Oberon tightened their cloaks against the chill of the early morning and headed toward the manor of Lord Llandon.

They passed a narrow lane before they came to a stone wall about waist high. There was no gate, only a stone archway extending from the wall. A stone path wound around a dried creek bed. An oak tree drooped over the path, dropping its acorns on the walkway.

"Halt, state your business." Two soldiers in silver helmets lowered their lances at the front door.

"Two travelers seeking a word with Lord Llandon," Eonder said.

"His Excellency is much too busy with important matters," one guard said. "You will have to schedule an appointment."

"Our business is most urgent." Eonder removed his green felt hat, revealing snow white hair. "Tell him his former employer has come to pay him a visit."

The two guards looked at each other before opening the wooden door of the manor of Lord Llandon. Inside was a galley of armor. Hanging from the wall were bucklers and long shields, circular shields made of wood and iron, pikes and crossbows, pole-axes, and iron swords of various lengths.

The two guards knocked on the door. "Go away. I do not want to be disturbed."

"Your Excellency, you have two visitors on urgent business to see you," one guard said.

"I'll determine what is urgent."

The guards swung open the door and Eonder and Oberon stepped in. A man with pink jowls and droopy eyes sat slumped over a large polished oak desk. Rolled parchments and papers lay spread out on the table. "If you must annoy me, be quick about it," the man said without looking up.

The guards closed the door behind them, leaving Eonder and Oberon standing in the room with the man with pink cheeks. "Hello, Llandon," Eonder said.

The man dropped the quill in his hand when he recognized the voice. His pink face turned white.

There was a moment of silence as Llandon lifted his head and stared at Eonder and his broad companion. "Uh...this is not a good time for me. I am quite busy."

"Yes, I can see that you are. Have we disturbed you?" Eonder said.

Llandon grabbed some scrolls on the table and pushed them into a drawer. "No, no...I mean, yes. Maybe it is best to reschedule. How about next Thursday?"

Eonder grinned. "Oh, we will not be long. We will let you get back to your official duties." Eonder stroked his beard. "Congratulations, by the way, on your promotion. I hear you are now steward of Helgath."

"Thank you. It has been years of hard work. I am not one to blow my own horn, as you know. Fortune smiled on me when she noticed my exceptional talents..." Llandon closed his mouth. Drops of perspiration formed on his forehead.

"Llandon, I remember when you were a squire. I tried to teach you that diligence and patience would bring its own reward. But you were brash and pompous, and had no regard for others."

Color returned to Llandon's whitened face, turning pink, then red. "I do not have to listen to you, old man. I am in charge here."

Eonder took one step toward Llandon, gripping his walking stick. "There is a way that seems right to a man, but the end leads to destruction."

Llandon jumped to his feet. "Guards!" The door burst open as the two guards rushed in to see what Llandon was shouting about.

"Arrest them," Llandon smirked.

As the two guards pointed their lances, Oberon reached out with his big hands and grabbed them by their collars and brought their two heads together. The metal helmets clanked. The guards slumped to the floor.

Llandon's Revenge

CHAPTER 6

Oberon slammed the door shut tight. He took a spear off the wall and jammed it through the door handle. "That should hold him for awhile. Llandon is too fat to climb through the window."

"Thank you, Oberon. Go back to The Lion's Paw and get Marallon and Gwendolyn. Take them to your ship, then escort Ben to his shack on the shoreline. Tell him he can be of great service to the king."

"It will be as you ask, sire. But where will you be?"

"I have to meet a friend. Take your ship to the Tip of Bregan. I will send word to you there."

Eonder watched Oberon exit the walkway before he turned down the cobblestone road and entered the narrow lane.

Oberon's large frame burst through the door of The Lion's Paw. Gwendolyn and Marallon had just finished breakfast. Ben was sitting by the fire. "Grab your belongings. We must leave now!" Gwendolyn, Marallon, and Ben all jumped in their chairs as they were startled by Oberon's sudden entry and booming voice.

Angwin entered from the kitchen. "What is going on out here?"

Oberon stepped into the middle of the room. "I am not used to giving an order twice. I said, 'Grab your belongings,' now!"

Gwendolyn, Marallon and Ben scurried up the steps to their rooms.

Angwin put his hands on his hips. "What is all the ruckus about?"

"There was some trouble with Llandon. Eonder said to take these three to safety." Oberon put his big hand on Angwin's shoulders. "I am afraid we have put you in a bit of a bind."

"Oh, never mind that. Me and the missus will be just fine."

Oberon took out a gold coin and laid it on the table. "It was good to see you again, old friend."

"Friends of King William are always welcome here," Angwin said.

Gwendolyn had changed into her tan deerskin britches and linen top. Her leather pack and bow and quiver were strapped over her shoulder. She entered the dining room before Marallon and Ben came down the stairs.

"Is my grandfather with you?" Gwendolyn held the note from Eonder in her hand.

"No, he is not, child. But he is part of the reason we must make haste," Oberon said. "Angwin, is there a back door we can leave by?"

"This way." Angwin led them to a back entrance. Oberon opened the door to a deserted alleyway. "Follow this alley. It will lead to a narrow street. Turn right. After a few paces you will come to the back of the courtyard and the market vendors."

Oberon nodded to Angwin as he guided the others into the alley. Gwendolyn turned to Angwin before he closed the back door. "What about my horse?"

"Mother and I will take good care of her until you return."

Oberon smiled at Gwendolyn. "Now, we must be going. Quietly, but swiftly."

They followed Angwin's instructions and came to the back of the courtyard. Vendors had already set up their carts and had begun to pitch their wares. Oberon held up his hand. The others stopped. "Blend in with the customers. But stay together."

A woman with a scarf on her head stepped in front of Marallon. "Have you ever seen potatoes like this?" she said as she shoved a potato at Marallon's face. "It will make for a good stew."

Oberon stepped between Marallon and the woman. "We need no potatoes today." Oberon put his arm around Marallon. "Ben, hold onto Gwendolyn and follow me."

Oberon pressed on through the masses of people. His size created an open space for the others to follow.

Oberon looked out over the crowd and saw an empty cart leaving the courtyard on the cobblestone road that lead to the city gate.

"Hurry, this way." Oberon caught up to the cart and lifted Gwendolyn and Marallon onto the open back. The driver turned to look. Oberon waved. The driver scratched his head and continued on.

Oberon and Ben walked on each side of the cart while the cart passed the sentry. The iron city gate was open and they passed through without drawing attention.

The driver of the cart steered his horse east from the city of Helgath. "Do you know a way down to the ocean?" Oberon said to Ben.

"There is a trail just ahead that can take us to my place and the sea."

Oberon lifted Gwendolyn and Marallon off the cart. Ben pushed through scrub brush onto a sandy path. Ocean waves could be seen below. "We better hurry. The tide is coming in," Ben said. The water was up to Gwendolyn's knees by the time Ben lead them through a tunnel that opened out to huge, black rocks.

A wave crashed against the rocks sending salt spray into their faces. "This way," Ben said. They clamored over more rocks onto a stretch of sand. Ben's wooden shack sat tucked against the cliff wall, protected from the ocean surf. "I would invite you in, but it would be a bit crowded."

Oberon noticed a rowboat leaning against the shack. "That will get us to my ship."

"But the tide is coming in," Ben said.

"I can row against the waves. May we borrow your boat?"

"Yes, of course. I will go with you." Ben and Oberon carried the boat over the rocks and down to where the waves splashed up on the sand. Gwendolyn, Marallon, and Ben shifted positions to make room for Oberon to get in after he pushed the boat into the tide.

Oberon heaved the oars into the breaking waves. He strained with every stroke, until the rowboat made it past the crashing waves.

He steered South, toward the pier of the city of Helgath. A sail appeared on the horizon. Flying high upon the mast was a flag of a golden lion, the symbol of King William. Yellow-green, blue-red, and orange-gold shields lined the side of the curved hull ship.

"She is a beautiful ship. I long to sail the seas in a vessel so fine," Ben said.

"Come with us," Gwendolyn said.

"I believe I may have a better plan." Oberon stopped rowing. "Ben, do you pledge your allegiance to King William?"

"I do."

"Then you can be of great help to your king. Watch for naval ships that do not hoist the flag of the golden lion."

"I will do as you say."

Oberon called out to The Morning Star as they approached. "Oh, hoy. Three to board." Two sailors peered over the rail and lowered a rope ladder over the side.

Gwendolyn hugged Ben's neck. "Thank you for helping me. I hope I will see your granddaughter someday."

"I hope so, too, lass. God speed to you." Ben turned his rowboat back toward the shore and his shack.

***

The door of The Lion's Paw flung open. Four soldiers brandishing pikes burst in, followed by Lord Llandon in a fur-trimmed coat. "Where are they?" Llandon screamed.

"Where are who?" Angwin was in the dining area cleaning up the breakfast plates of his guests.

Llandon walked up to Angwin and pointed his finger in Angwin's face. "I know they were here."

Angwin put down the plates. "Again, I ask, who are you talking about?"

Llandon waved his finger. "The old man and the large one. Do you deny that they were here?"

"No. I do not deny it. They are my friends."

Llandon smirked. "Then you will be arrested for treason."

Angwin laughed and picked up the plates. "Treason? For showing loyalty to King William? There is only one true lord over this city."

Llandon's jowls puffed out. He knocked the plates across the room. Spittle came out of his mouth and dribbled down his chin as he shouted, "Guards, arrest this man."

Two guards seized Angwin by his arms as Angwin's wife appeared from the kitchen. She hurried to her husband. "Angwin, are you all right?"

"Take care of things, mother. I will not be gone long." The guards jerked Angwin out the door.

The Queen's Chair

CHAPTER 7

Mortimer hopped out of bed with the pink light of dawn. He threw on the navy outfit he wore the day before and wrapped the leather belt his mother had made around his waist. After placing his special pointy stick through the loop, Mortimer put on the golden helmet. He shoved his leather shield into his pack and bolted out the bedroom door.

Mortimer hurried down the hallway to the Banquet Room and threw open the doors. "I am ready," he shouted.

The room was empty.

Mortimer left the Banquet Room for the Queen's Throne Room. He knocked on the door. There was no answer. He pulled the door open a crack and poked his head in. "Hello. Is anyone here?" Mortimer shivered, due to the eerie silence of being alone in the large stone chamber, and then because only one torch lit the room.

Mortimer crept deeper into the room. "Hello. Anyone?" His voice squeaked. "Maybe no one else is awake yet." He approached the Queen's throne in the shadows and stood in front of it. He looked again throughout the room, walked around the throne, hesitated, then jumped up into the seat of the throne.

The seat, headrest, and legs were formed from solid gold. At the base of the four legs it appeared that someone had tried to chisel off a decoration. Mortimer looked close. It could be the face of a lion.

He ran his hands over the golden armrests. The smooth metal warmed to his touch, and he remembered holding the gold in Gharma's cave. He sat up straight. "I am King Mortimer," he said, trying to make his voice deeper, "and you will do as I say."

All of a sudden, Mortimer felt bony fingers dig into his shoulder.

"No. You will do as I say." Ghimel stepped out of the shadows. "Is this how you killed my twin brother, Gharma, by creeping up on him in the dark? Were you looking to steal the golden crown for yourself? Do you think you can ascend the throne?"

Mortimer squirmed under Ghimel's grasp and slid out of the chair. "I was just pretending...I did not mean any harm."

Ghimel's pointed nose almost hit Mortimer in the eye. "I know what you were doing, and you can never have it."

Mortimer leaned back from Ghimel's glare. "I do not know what you mean."

Ghimel's eyes bulged. "Only the wise and worthy can sit upon its splendor. Many would kill for it. It would be a shame if some harm came to you. Now, get out of here."

Mortimer backed away.

"And remember, I will be watching you." Ghimel's bony finger pointed at Mortimer.

Mortimer ran out the door and down the hallway. He burst into his room and flopped on the bed. The pointy stick on his belt loop dug into his hip. He sat up and tore the belt from his waist, throwing it on the couch, then pulled the pack with the leather shield from his back and flung it across the room. He slammed the golden helmet onto the floor.

A knock sounded at the door.

"Go away," Mortimer sniveled.

"Are you ill, sire? I heard a thud." It was Baldor, Mortimer's servant.

Mortimer wiped his nose. "I am fine. I just...dropped my pack."

"May I come in and clean up the mess, sire?"

Mortimer wiped his eyes and opened the door.

Baldor crossed the room to the jumbled pack and set it on the bed with care. He picked up the belt and the pointed stick, along with the golden helmet, and lay them next to the pack. Once done, he opened the windows. "The fresh air will revive you, sire. A splash of water on your face and you will be ready for breakfast." Baldor fluffed the pillows, straightened the sheets, and then closed the door as he left the room.

Mortimer sat on the edge of the bed. He touched his leather pack, letting his fingers feel the shape of the shield inside. He lifted the pointy stick. "Who am I kidding? I am no king."

Just then, the falcon that had appeared earlier, flew up to the window and perched on the sill.

"Have you come to mock me, also?" Mortimer said. The bird tilted his head to the right.

"I bet you would fly away and leave me if I got too close." The falcon blinked.

Mortimer walked to the window. "I bet you would take wing if I stuck out my hand," he said as he extended his right hand. "I bet you will bolt before you rest on my arm." Mortimer straightened his arm. The bird hopped onto his sleeve.

Mortimer froze. He had not expected the falcon to jump onto his arm. He imagined the bird's sharp talons shredding his sleeve and ripping his flesh. He shook that thought from his mind. "Maybe you are hungry?" Mortimer looked around the room, but there was no food there.

Baldor knocked on the door. "The Queen requests your presence for breakfast, sire."

"I will be right there." Mortimer lifted his arm so the bird could hop onto the windowsill. "I will be back after breakfast and bring you some meat. You can be my friend." Mortimer turned to look once more at the falcon sitting in his window before he closed the door and skipped down the hall to the Banquet Room.

Mortimer's Quest

CHAPTER 8

Queen Valora was spreading butter on a muffin when Mortimer burst into the Banquet Room. "Here I am," Mortimer said.

"Well, there is my little man," the Queen said. "Come sit by me."

Mortimer pulled out a chair to the right of Queen Valora. Ghimel sat across the table from Mortimer and glared while Mortimer cut a piece of ham.

"Are you ready for your adventure?" the Queen said.

Mortimer's mouth was stuffed with a slice of bread and a glob of boysenberry jam. "Yes," he mumbled.

Queen Valora straightened her back. "Here are my orders. Ghimel, you will lead Mortimer and a band of my soldiers through the territory of Hamendal. The river will be your fastest course. Head west toward the Black Mountains. Mortimer, you are to lead them to Gharma's cave, find my crown, and bring it back to me."

"It will be as you say, my Queen," Ghimel said.

Mortimer started to open his mouth, caught a glimpse of Ghimel's narrow eyes, and closed it.

"Ghimel, see that all preparations are completed. Meet me in the courtyard in one half hour."

"As you wish, my Queen." Ghimel left Queen Valora and Mortimer alone.

"There are some final details that I need to discuss."

Mortimer smacked his lips on the boysenberry jam. "I am listening."

"The crown is...special to me. It is most important that I have it."

Mortimer put down the bread and jam. "I will bring it back to you."

Queen Valora smiled. "Good. I knew I could depend on you." She leaned toward Mortimer. "When I have my crown, I will need a prince. Someone brave and loyal."

Mortimer puffed out his chest. He thought of sitting on a throne of his own next to the Queen's with a crown on his head and a scepter like Queen Valora's. They would live forever, and rule a perfect kingdom.

"Something is not quite right." The Queen squinted at Mortimer. "Your outfit is missing something."

"I have a present for you." The Queen lifted a navy velvet hat from under the table. It was shaped like a muffin rising in the oven, and had a peacock feather stuck in the side. "This is a symbol of a trusted envoy. I would like you to wear it."

Queen Valora stood and placed the navy hat on his head. "I want you to be my Ambassador. There are many enemies to my throne."

"I will protect you with my life... and my sword." Mortimer felt for the pointed stick on his belt, then remembered he had left it in his room. "There is something I need to get."

The Queen narrowed her eyes. "Well, hurry up. Meet me in the courtyard."

Mortimer was at the door when he heard the Queen holler, "And do not dawdle."

Mortimer ran down the hallway and flung open the door to his room. The pointy stick and his pack were still on his bed where he left them. He saw the golden helmet by his pillow, and remembered Eonder's words about the helmet protecting his thoughts. Mortimer stuck out his chest. "Humph, I don't need Eonder to protect me." He tied the leather belt that held the stick around his waist and put the pack with the leather shield over his shoulder.

Mortimer felt a breeze blow through his window. The falcon, he had forgotten to bring some meat. Mortimer went to the window and looked up and then down. The bird was nowhere to be found.

Mortimer shrugged his shoulders, then hurried out the door and down the hallway. He bounded down the steps of the eastern tower and pushed open the wooden door to the courtyard.

Mortimer saw peasants rolling barrels into a cart near the stables. Another cart had been loaded with three wooden canoes. Ten soldiers with silver conical helmets stood at attention, holding the reins of their horses. Swords hung from belts on their left sides and in their right hands, each gripped an iron spear.

Queen Valora was speaking to a man near one of the carts. Mortimer ran up to her. "I did not dawdle."

When the man stepped to the side, Mortimer saw that it was Ghimel with a sneer on his face.

"I am depending on you to bring me my crown," the Queen said, "and Ghimel, this child is important to me. See that he is returned safely."

Ghimel stepped behind Mortimer and put his hands on Mortimer's shoulders. "I will personally watch over him, my Queen."

Queen Valora adjusted Mortimer's navy velvet cap. "Be careful. There are many enemies who seek to take away my throne."

Mortimer wanted to puff out his chest, or raise his sword, or bow down in allegiance to the Queen but with Ghimel's hands on his shoulders, he felt small and inferior.

Ghimel hopped onto the lead horse as he threw back his long green coat, trimmed with black fur. A stable- hand helped Mortimer into his saddle. Ghimel raised his right arm and the gate of the White Castle lifted.

Mortimer found himself riding behind Ghimel and two soldiers as the troop proceeded out of the castle courtyard. Ghimel held his head high as soldiers at the gate saluted.

Mortimer remembered riding on these same cobble stones with Gwendolyn. So much had changed since that day when they approached the White Castle.

He looked behind to see the iron gate of the castle being lowered. A grey cloud passed in front of the sun, darkening the ground before him. Mortimer shivered. He was headed back to the Black Mountains, back to Gharma's cave.

Storms and Serpents

CHAPTER 9

The turrets of the White Castle disappeared from Mortimer's view as the troop headed North through the country of Hamendal. He hoped they would pass near the garden where he and Gwendolyn had stopped on their way to the White Castle.

Mortimer remembered the red apple he picked that day. It was the most delicious fruit he had ever eaten. His stomach growled. Oh, if he could just have another bite of one of those apples.

Dark clouds continued to gather from the East. The cobblestone road had merged into a dirt path. Ghimel raised his hand to stop the troop when he came to a fork in the road. "Two of you men take the cart with the barrels and stay on the northern road. Meet up with us by sundown tomorrow at our camp at the Marsh of Moel Non."

Mortimer wondered why Ghimel would want to camp near a marsh, but before he could come up with an answer, Ghimel had the remaining troop moving northeast on the other path. The dirt road passed a grove of elm trees and opened to a small river. Ghimel raised his hand again. The cart with the canoes and soldiers stopped.

"Why do we have to stop here?" Mortimer said to the guard riding next to him.

"We will take the boats up Pen Dinar, the Wide River, to Loch Elsinor," the guard said.

"Wide River? It does not look wide to me," Mortimer said.

The guard joined the others to lift the three canoes off the wagon.

"Stay here with our horses." Ghimel pointed his finger at a soldier. "We will return in two days time."

The driver nodded his head.

The guards carried the boats over gravel that lay at the water's edge, and then lowered them into the river. Mortimer saw that one canoe was filled in the center with bed rolls and leather packs. He stepped into an empty boat.

"Anxious to retrieve the crown, are you?" Ghimel lifted his long green robe and climbed into Mortimer's canoe. "I promised the Queen I would keep an eye on you. It would be a pity if any harm came to you." His lips parted into another sneer.

Two guards pushed the boat with supplies away from the shore, leaving the other soldiers to select a boat. Four hopped into empty canoes. Two guards remained standing on the shore.

"If you want to stay in the employ of the Queen, I suggest you serve her Counselor." Ghimel sat in the canoe with arms folded.

The guards labored to get the canoe heavy with Mortimer and Ghimel afloat. They paddled with quick strokes to catch up to the other boats.

Ghimel folded a piece of animal fur and lay it on the birch beam that crossed the boat. He then adjusted himself into a comfortable position opposite from Mortimer.

Mortimer pretended to be interested in the shoreline as the river grew wider, but he could feel Ghimel's eyes watching him. He lowered his hand into the river and let the cool, green water rush over his open palm.

"You best be careful. You do not know what lurks in this river." Ghimel smirked as Mortimer jerked his hand back into the boat.

Thunder rumbled across the sky. Faint drops of rain left tiny ripples in the water. Wind whipped over the trees along the bank, forming waves on the Pen Dinar and the rain became heavier. Soon Mortimer was soaked to the skin.

Ghimel motioned for the boats to make for the western shore. Pine and fir trees lining the bank would offer some protection from the storm. The soldiers pulled the boats up the gravel bank. One soldier handed Mortimer a wool blanket from the bed roll so he could wrap it around his shoulders. Mortimer sat down on a bed of pine needles with his back against a tall, wide spreading pine.

The lightening flashed across the dark clouds. Rain came down in torrents. Water fell from the branches over Mortimer onto his neck and rolled down his back. He shivered as he huddled his knees closer to his body and pulled the blanket over his head.

An hour passed. The wind died down and the rain stopped. Ghimel motioned for the guards to put the boats back into the water. Mortimer kept the blanket wrapped around him as he climbed back into the canoe.

The Pen Dinar River fed into Loch Elsinor, a large, green water lake. The boats passed by branches that had been torn from their trees during the storm as the guards steered on a northwest course.

"I have heard there is a giant serpent in this loch," Ghimel said to Mortimer. "You see two humps in the water before it rises up to eat you." Ghimel waited for a response.

Mortimer looked away as he scooted closer to the middle of the boat. He did not want Ghimel to see him afraid.

As the afternoon sun cast long shadows across the loch, Mortimer noticed some movement ahead in the water. The boats were headed straight for it. Mortimer squinted his eyes to get a better look. "I saw the sea serpent," Mortimer screamed.

The guards stopped paddling to look at Mortimer. Ghimel laughed, and reached down into the water to pull out a bent tree branch. "Look, the boy is afraid of a twig."

He hissed. The guards laughed, then continued paddling their canoes.

Mortimer lowered his head in embarrassment. He pulled the blanket tighter around him and sighed.

The Golden Crown

CHAPTER 10

It was dusk when the canoes landed at the northwest shore of Loch Elsinor. The guards carried the boats into a grove of willow trees. Pale-green moss hung from the tree branches like strings of cobwebs.

Mortimer looked to the West. The sun had started to dip below the Black Mountains. The jagged peak of Mt. Fangor rose up against the horizon. It would be half a days journey to reach the base of the mountains.

The guards had gone off to gather sticks for a fire. Mortimer sat down on some soft grass and leaned against a pine tree.

"What do you think you are doing?" Ghimel said.

Mortimer sat up straight.

"Go find wood for the fire." Ghimel looked up at the setting sun. "But you better hurry. Mordrum, the creature that stalks Moel Non, comes out at night. He loves to chew on the bones of young urchins."

Mortimer saw a guard through the trees and ran to join him. Mortimer heard Ghimel laughing.

Several guards started a blazing fire in a cleared area and prepared food for dinner. After he ate, Mortimer laid his velvet hat on the grass as a pillow and curled up to go to sleep. The wind blew through the trees, causing the mossy strands on the tree branches to lift in the air. Mortimer pulled the blanket over his shoulders and closed his eyes.

His dreams disturbed him. A black figure lurked in the woods of Moel Non. It had moss for hair and yellow eyes. It sniffed the ground, coming closer, even closer to the camp.

"Get up. Did you plan on sleeping all morning?" Ghimel stood over Mortimer. "We must reach the mountain pass by mid-morning."

They ate breakfast in a hurry and put out the fire. The guards were ready to march. As the men headed out of the Willow Grove, Mortimer found a perfect walking stick. Ghimel was in the back of the group, so Mortimer stayed near the front.

The ground softened as they left the willows. Mortimer watched mud squirt around his shoes with each step he took. A gray mist hung close to the ground and a strange smell like turnips cooking made Mortimer's nose itch.

"Where are we?" Mortimer said to the guard walking near him.

"We are in the Marsh of Moel Non."

"What is this?" Mortimer pointed to the fog that had surrounded all of them.

"It is the breath of Mordrum," the guard whispered, "but you must not speak of it."

"What is Mordrum?"

"Mordrum is a goblin, a spook to these parts." The guard huffed. "And you're going to bring him right to us." The guard scurried away toward the front of the line.

The gray mist became thicker. "I cannot see where I am going," Mortimer said.

"Hold my hand young one." Mortimer saw a hand extend through the fog.

"Wait. How do I know I can trust you?"

"My name is Harlech, and I will see that no harm comes to you."

Mortimer grabbed his hand and continued through the mist. All of a sudden, Mortimer heard a scream. He squeezed Harlech's hand tighter.

"Stay back." Harlech held out his arm.

It was then that Mortimer saw the soldier, who had been leading the way, up to his waist in brown muck.

Ghimel arrived. "Why did we stop?" Ghimel noticed the guard struggling in the ooze. "Ah, you seem to have stepped into a bog."

"Do something. Get me out of here," the guard pleaded as he reached out both his arms.

"I am afraid there is nothing I can do."

"Is not anyone going to help him?" Mortimer said as he looked at the faces of the men. The other soldiers stayed back. Mortimer looked at Harlech. "Hold my hand tight. Do not let go." Harlech nodded and gripped Mortimer's hand.

Mortimer leaned forward, holding out his walking stick, extending it across the muck. The guard reached for the stick. His fingers had it, then slipped off. The ooze was almost up to his shoulders. His eyes filled with terror as he reached out his hand again before the weight of the bog pulled his head under. The brown muck bubbled as it closed over the top of the guard's silver helmet.

"We have wasted enough time here," Ghimel said. "You, what is your name?" Ghimel pointed to Harlech.

"Harlech, my lord."

"You will lead us to the mountain pass."

"Yes, my lord." Harlech pulled Mortimer back onto firmer ground and let go of his grip.

At last, the morning sun thinned the mist over the Marsh of Moel Non. Harlech guided the men out of the marsh and onto a dusty trail headed northwest. Mortimer stayed close to Harlech as the Black Mountains loomed closer.

By mid-morning the group started ascending the rocky trail. Mortimer's legs ached. Before, he was on horseback when he had come up these mountains with Eonder. Now he appreciated the labor of the horses, when they had climbed up this steep path.

At noon they stopped for water and lunch where the path leveled. Ghimel approached Mortimer. "Boy, where is my brother's cave?"

Mortimer looked left and right, trying to remember. "This is where we fought Gharma. His cave was..." Mortimer pointed south, "right over there."

A pile of large boulders lay where Mortimer pointed.

"Is this my brother's burial pile after you ambushed and murdered him?" Ghimel hissed.

"There was nothing to bury," Mortimer said. "He just disappeared in a puff of smoke. These rocks fell when Eonder tapped the cave with his stick."

"Remove the rocks." Ghimel said to the guards.

It took two men to lift the first few boulders and throw them to the side. The men worked faster when they saw the hole of the cave. A foul stench came from the opening.

Ghimel pushed the guards aside when the hole was large enough to crawl through. "I will go." Ghimel crawled over the top of the rocks and down into the cave. "Send the boy in," he called over his shoulder.

Mortimer stood next to Ghimel inside Gharma's cave. Hazy light filtered through the boulders into the entrance of the cave. Ghimel grabbed Mortimer's left arm. "Show me where the crown is."

Mortimer winced from the pain of Ghimel's grip. "It was near the back, on a pile of gold. I used my sword to light the way." Mortimer pulled the pointy stick out of his belt loop. Nothing happened. "That is odd. It gave a blue light before."

Ghimel snorted. "You will have to find it in the dark." He pushed Mortimer forward.

Mortimer squinted to see as he held out his hand in front of him. He shuffled his feet in the darkness of the cave. He continued to move forward, one slow step after another.

The air was hot and foul. Mortimer felt the slimy side of the wall and something slithered over his hand. "Eww." He took four steps, and heard the crunch of bones under his feet. Mortimer sensed small animals scurrying in the dark and heard the sound of rats. He jumped backward as one crawled over his foot. He stumbled into a large pile of metal objects.

Ghimel let go of Mortimer as Mortimer began to fall. Something hard poked Mortimer in the ribs. He felt the smooth exterior of the objects, and knew where he had landed.

"Where are you, boy?" Ghimel said.

Mortimer tried to slip small gold coins into his pack. He remembered from the time he was here with Eonder that the pile consisted of golden boxes filled with sapphires, golden pendants trimmed with emeralds, thousands of gold coins, and on top of the pile, a golden crown fit for a king.

Mortimer had a fistful of coins in his right hand when he felt Ghimel's icy grip on his shoulder.

"What are you doing, boy?"

"I...I was looking for the crown." Mortimer reached for the top of the pile and felt the shape of the crown. He thrust it into Ghimel's hand. "Here it is."

Ghimel let go of his hold on Mortimer. "I have it. I have found the crown. Quick, lead me to the entrance." Ghimel grabbed Mortimer's arm as they turned and shuffled toward the pinpoint of light now dim ahead of them.

Ghimel pushed ahead of Mortimer once they reached the light coming through the opening, and scampered over the rocks into the daylight.

Ghimel held the crown up so the light of the sun caught its beauty. The crown, made of polished gold, had an intricate design carved in the forehead band, inlaid with diamonds and pearls. Ghimel ran his fingers over every inch of the crown, then slipped it inside a velvet pouch he carried inside his coat.

"We will return to camp," Ghimel said.

The guards looked at each other. "What about the treasure?" a guard said.

"I have what I came for. Spend the night here if you like. Or return in the morning for the trinkets." Ghimel started walking down the path.

The sun had started its descent in the western sky, and a northern wind had picked up. The prospect of a cold, fireless night on Mount Fangor caused the guards to trudge behind Ghimel.

Mortimer stayed close to Harlech, but kept his eye on Ghimel, who carried the golden crown. The wind blasted from the north, whipping dust from the trail into Mortimer's eye. It was on this trail, when Mortimer devised a plan to bring the crown to Queen Valora.

Mortimer Meets a Friend

As Ghimel walked ten paces in front of everyone else, Mortimer could hear some of the guards grumbling. Grit formed on Mortimer's face and neck from the dirt of the trail.

"My feet are aching."

"Quit your yapping."

"Why not grab the gold while we were there?"

"Now we have to go back tomorrow."

"Quit your yapping."

The troop approached the bog on the border of the Marsh of Moel Non. The early evening sun cast menacing shadows over the marsh.

A falcon lifted off from the willows of the marsh and rose high into the sky before descending on the group with a short screech. The bird headed straight for Ghimel, who ducked just in time as he fell to the ground.

When the falcon landed on Mortimer's shoulder, he was quite surprised that the bird from his windowsill found him so far from home.

Ghimel struggled to get up, but he was tangled in his long coat. "Help me up, you fools." Two guards hurried over to lift Ghimel under his arms.

Mortimer snickered.

Ghimel stomped to where Mortimer stood and put his bony finger in Mortimer's face. "Do you mock me?"

The falcon on Mortimer's shoulder flapped its wings and snapped its sharp beak at Ghimel's finger.

Ghimel pulled his hand back, and glared at Mortimer. "You will get yours," he said. "You, and your bird." Ghimel pointed once more at Mortimer before he turned to head down the path through the bog.

Harlech looked at the falcon on Mortimer's shoulder. "When did you learn to tame a hunting bird?" he said.

Mortimer's first reaction was to make up a story about the many wild animals he had tamed. But he stopped. "It just found me one day, then flew into my window."

Harlech patted him on the head. "Well, keep it close by. It is a good omen."

The guards looked at Mortimer with respect, but kept their distance from the bird.

With the fog burned off, it was easier to follow the narrow path through the bog. Mortimer stayed close to Harlech, and the falcon stayed perched on Mortimer's shoulder. Mortimer saw the walking stick on the path, the one he had used that morning to try to save the drowning guard. He bent down to pick it up, even though the stick was covered in the dark, brown slime of the bog.

Mortimer, Harlech, and the other guards soon made their safe way to the camp in the willow grove of the Marsh of Moel Non. The horse-drawn cart and its driver then arrived as a guard started a fire.

Night began to fall. As the stars started to twinkle above, Mortimer noticed a wineskin being passed from guard to guard. Mortimer ate his meat and bread in silence, offering some to the falcon, who snatched it into its beak and swallowed.

Mortimer wondered where Ghimel was, for he had not seen him at the campsite. Mortimer's plan could not work if Ghimel had the crown, or presented it to the Queen himself. The thought made Mortimer quite angry. He picked up the walking stick and hurled it into the fire. At once, bright flames leapt from the stick, making the guards sitting closest to the fire fall backward.

"Eh, what did you go and do that for?"

"You nearly singed my eyebrows off."

Mortimer backed away from the angry guards. "Sorry."

The guards scowled and passed the wineskin again, ignoring Mortimer as he continued to move away from them, until he was out of sight.

When he thought he was far enough from the camp, Mortimer took the gold from his backpack that he was able to grab in Gharma's cave. Two golden rings and five gold coins. Mortimer was examining the coins, when he heard chanting. It was from one voice, and it was just ahead.

Mortimer crept through the willows, using the light of the full moon to step over those branches or twigs that could snap or crack. He could see a man, standing on a grassy mound, with his back to Mortimer. The man reached into his long coat and held up something toward the moon. Even in the pale light, Mortimer could see it was the glorious golden crown.

"Marewych, Borewych, Alcat Anir. Formed at the dawn of time for the one who would rule forever."

Mortimer felt his mind being drawn into the moonlight chant.

The falcon lifted off his shoulder and flew deeper into the woods.

"Wait. Where are you going? Come back here." Mortimer whispered as he reached for the bird. Mortimer looked one more time at Ghimel and the crown, then turned to run after the falcon who was flying in the night sky just above the tree-tops. He ran faster, crashing through willow branches and wiping the mossy strands from his face.

The falcon glided to a stop just as Mortimer came to a small clearing in the willow grove. He bent over and panted, trying to catch his breath. When he looked up, he noticed a hooded figure sitting on a white horse. The hooded figure held out his arm, and the falcon perched upon it.

"That is my bird," Mortimer wheezed.

"Your bird? I would say the bird returned to me." The man on the horse pulled back the hood of his cape to reveal a long, white beard.

"Eonder." Mortimer could not believe his eyes. He stood up straight and said, "What are you doing out here?"

"I could ask the same of you."

"I...I came with them." Mortimer pointed back to the camp.

"And why are you here in my Willow Grove?"

Mortimer hung his head.

Eonder got off his horse, still holding the falcon. "Come here, Mortimer."

Mortimer did not move.

"Did you lead them to Gharma's cave?"

Mortimer did not answer, but remembered he was still holding the gold coins in his fist.

"I see you are wearing a different hat from the helmet I gave you."

Mortimer reached up to feel the navy velvet cap on his head. He felt a flush of embarrassment, then stuck out his chin. "It means I am an ambassador for...oh, never mind."

Eonder stepped toward Mortimer. "Have you forgotten what I told you?"

"I have not forgotten that you left me."

Eonder looked at Mortimer with gentle eyes. "But I have never left you, nor forsaken you."

Mortimer blinked his eyes hard, trying to keep the tears from coming out.

Eonder took two more steps closer. "Would you like to take a bite of your apple?"

"What?"

"The apple in your pack. The one you took from my garden."

Mortimer remembered he had picked an extra red apple when he was in the garden with Gwendolyn. But he had forgotten he had put it in his backpack. Mortimer reached into his pack to put the gold in his fist out of sight, and to pull out the red apple. A gold coin tumbled from his hand and fell to the ground. Quick as he could, Mortimer covered it with his foot. He held the apple as he looked at Eonder.

"You might as well eat it before it rots. All things spoil that stay long with the Queen."

Mortimer huffed and turned his head away.

Eonder climbed back onto his horse. "Besides, she will never allow anything red in her presence."

"What is that supposed to mean?"

"You will have to ask her, yourself." Eonder turned the horse's head with the reins. "You must choose who you will give your allegiance to. I will be waiting for you at Gwendolyn's cabin in the Narrow Wood." With that, Eonder rode off through the willows, the falcon still on his arm.

Mortimer lifted his foot and picked up the gold coin which he put, along with the apple, into his pack. He stood in the clearing, watching the sky turn dark as clouds passed in front of the moon. Mortimer felt a tear fall from his eye and race down his cheek. He turned and shuffled back to camp.

Treachery

CHAPTER 12

By the time Mortimer returned to camp, the wineskin had been emptied and lay on the ground. The guards slumped in slumber near the fire. Snores and snortles mingled with the crackle of the burning logs.

Mortimer pulled the blanket over his head and closed his eyes. His sleep was fitful. In the shadows of his dreams he saw Ghimel place the crown on his own high and narrow forehead. At once, Ghimel grew twenty feet in height. Queen Valora appeared and raised her scepter. Lightening flashed, then both she and Ghimel turned to snakes, as they writhed and wrestled for control of the crown.

Cold air crept under Mortimer's blanket and gripped his toes and knees. He tried to pull the blanket tighter, but woke up when he felt his knees knocking together. The pink sky spread against the darkness. Mortimer got up to add some dried branches to the dying flame and glowing embers.

"Get up, you sluggards, there is work to be done." Ghimel stood in the center of camp shouting his order.

The soldiers struggled to rouse themselves and shake the grogginess from their heads.

"I said, 'Get up'." Ghimel kicked a guard who was still asleep.

The other guards jumped to their feet and stood at attention.

Ghimel circled the campfire, eyeing the guards. "You will go back to my brother's cave and load the gold into the cart. You will bring the treasure back to the castle. I have a list of every item that is in the cave, so if so much as one ring is missing, all of your heads will roll."

Mortimer saw the guards exchange worried looks. Then Mortimer wondered what Ghimel would do when he discovered the missing two rings and five gold coins in Mortimer's backpack.

Ghimel motioned to Harlech. "You will take me back to the castle." Then, Ghimel turned toward Mortimer and pointed a bony finger. "And you, will come with me, where I can keep on eye on you."

Mortimer heard the hiss of the flames as a guard doused the fire. His stomach grumbled, but he did not want to ask about breakfast. He knew he had the red apple in his backpack if he got more hungry.

As Mortimer walked to the boat over the stones at the edge of Loch Elsinor, he tripped over a rock and stumbled, knocking Ghimel into the canoe.

"You idiot. How dare you push me." Ghimel grabbed an oar from inside the canoe and swung at Mortimer.

The oar whooshed over Mortimer's head as he ducked.

Ghimel raised his arm to swing again, but Harlech reached up and grabbed Ghimel's wrist.

"The Queen said not to harm the boy."

Ghimel, with the oar in his hand, stood over Mortimer as he knelt on the rocks, one arm covering his head.

Ghimel's eyes bulged. He threw the oar onto the stones, saying, "You will both pay for your insolence."

Harlech picked up the oar and helped Mortimer into the canoe. Ghimel sat in the middle, arms folded across his chest. Harlech eased the boat into the water.

The trip back across the loch seemed longer than before. No one spoke a word. Harlech glanced back three or four times from the front of the canoe, to look at Mortimer.

Harlech paddled upstream on the Pen Dinar and pulled ashore at the spot in the elm trees where they had left the horses.

In Ghimel's haste to get out of the boat, he stepped into the river up to his knees. Water dripped from the bottom of his surcoat. Mortimer listened to Ghimel grumble as he stomped to where the horses were tied.

The guard who had stayed behind to watch the horses saw Ghimel approach. "Good day, my lord," he said.

Ghimel pushed past him, untied his horse, and rode off toward the White Castle.

Mortimer felt a sense of relief as he watched. Then he remembered that Ghimel had the golden crown.

"We must catch him," Mortimer shouted to Harlech.

"Why?"

"I...I think he is going to do something dreadful."

The guard tending the horses had a puzzled look as Mortimer and Harlech untied their mounts and galloped in pursuit of Ghimel.

As Mortimer and Harlech raced toward the White Castle, they could see the dust from Ghimel's horse in the distance. The iron gate of the White Castle lifted, and Ghimel passed through.

Soon, Mortimer and Harlech rode past the sentry and into the White Castle, too. Mortimer jumped down from his horse, and ran through the courtyard and up the stone steps to the inner chambers. He turned right at a hallway lined with torches and came to the large wooden doors of the Throne Room.

Mortimer pulled the bronze handle. The door did not open. He heard the same chanting as the night before in the willow grove. He pounded against the door until his hands throbbed.

"What are you doing?" It was one of Queen Valora's young maiden attendants.

"Where is the Queen?" Mortimer was near tears.

"She is in her chamber."

Mortimer took off for the Queen's room.

"But she is not to be disturbed."

Mortimer knocked on Queen Valora's door.

"Who dares disturb me?"

"It is Mortimer. Quick, your highness." Mortimer heard a key in the door before it opened. Queen Valora stood tall in the doorway.

"You are back sooner than I expected. Do you bring me word?"

Mortimer tried hard to compose himself, but blurted out, "Ghimel has the crown."

"What did you say?"

"I found the crown in Gharma's cave. Ghimel took it. He is locked in the Throne Room."

Queen Valora's eyes narrowed. She seemed to grow a foot taller as her shoulders raised. At once she marched down the hallway and pounded on the Throne Room door.

"Ghimel, open this door." She yanked the handle, but the door was barred from the inside. "Guards," Queen Valora yelled down both sides of the hallway. Four sentries responded with their pole-axes extended.

"You called, your Highness?"

"Break down this door."

Mortimer and Queen Valora stepped back as the sentries stepped forward. Their heavy ax heads dug into the thick wood. Mortimer's heart raced with each whack and thud.

Wood chunks from the heavy Throne Room door splayed in every direction. Sweat beaded on the faces of the sentries. A splintered hole appeared. A few more whacks and the hole grew wider.

The sentries lowered their shoulders and charged against the door. Metal hinges groaned. They charged again. The door crashed to the ground with a thud.

Mortimer peered around the back of Queen Valora into the dimly lit Throne Room.

The Queen and the Crown

Queen Valora stepped around the fallen door and into the Throne Room. The sentries took up positions around her with their pole-axes extended. Ghimel sat on the golden throne in the dim light of the room. The glorious crown sat radiant upon his head.

"I am the king," Ghimel said with a smirk.

"No, you are not." Queen Valora appeared calm.

Ghimel gripped the golden armrest tighter. "I have the crown."

"That does not make you king."

Ghimel stuck out his chin. "I have the crown. I have ascended to the throne. I rule the kingdom. I am the Chosen One."

Queen Valora chuckled. "The Chosen One? Do you think that by wearing the crown you fulfill the prophecy?"

Ghimel looked confused.

Queen Valora narrowed her eyes. "Guards, take away this impostor."

The sentries hesitated.

"I will have the head of anyone who defies me," the Queen screamed. The sentries jumped into action and surrounded Ghimel.

Ghimel gripped the throne tighter. "I am the king." The sentries pried his hands from the armrest and lifted him from the chair.

Ghimel squirmed to get free from their grasp. "I am the king. I am the king."

"Take him to the Block," the Queen said.

Ghimel managed to get one arm free from the sentry's hold, and lunged at Mortimer. "You have done this," he hissed.

Mortimer jumped back behind Queen Valora's long purple dress. The Queen's scepter came down with a crack on Ghimel's arm.

Ghimel howled.

"Guards, if he breaks loose again, your necks will be stretched on the gallows." The sentries nodded and made sure they had a firm grip on Ghimel. "And do shut him up."

A sentry's elbow smashed into Ghimel's mouth and his body went limp.

"I will take that." Queen Valora lifted the crown from Ghimel's head. His feet dragged on the floor as the sentries pulled him from the Throne Room down the stone hallway.

A crowd gathered in the courtyard at the sight of four sentries dragging the Queen's Advisor, followed by Queen Valora herself and a young boy. At the Northeast corner of the courtyard was a wooden platform raised about five feet off the ground. Wooden steps led up to the platform. A wicker basket was positioned on the opposite side of the platform.

A crowd formed around the Block. The sentries lifted Ghimel up the steps to a rectangular box of wood near the edge.

"Send for the Executioner," the Queen said.

A broad-shouldered man emerged from a door near the stables. The Executioner wore a brown leather vest, exposing thick, hairy arms. His head was covered in a black cloth with holes cut out for the eyes. His hands held a long shafted ax, sharpened at the blade.

The crowd gasped and parted to the left and right.

The Executioner made his way up the steps of the platform and stood to the left of the sentries. Ghimel began to stir and open his eyes. He shrieked and squirmed when he realized where he was.

"No, I am the king," Ghimel squealed.

The Executioner took a stretch of rope and a dirty rag from his waistband, and threw them at the sentries. One sentry took the rope and tied Ghimel's hands behind his back. Another took the rag and shoved it in Ghimel's mouth.

Queen Valora strode forward and raised her arms. The golden scepter and glorious crown glistened in the sunlight. "I am Queen Valora. Ruler of the East and Power of the West. Death will come to all who defy me, or dare to usurp my throne."

The crowd grew silent.

Ghimel was forced to kneel on the platform, his neck extended out on the rectangular block. The Executioner raised his ax high, then brought it down, swift and hard, as the Queen lowered her arm.

Some in the crowd gasped, others cheered as Ghimel's head dropped into the basket. Mortimer turned away. He felt sick.

"Take his body outside the walls for the birds to pick," the Queen said. She patted Mortimer on the head. "Do not be late for supper." Queen Valora lifted the train of her dress, turned on her heels, and strode to the stone staircase of the east tower.

Mortimer watched her walk away. His head felt dizzy and his knees weak. He bent over to vomit. With shaky steps, he made it to his room and fell on the bed.

He thought of Ghimel being dragged up the steps of the Block, and the Executioner's sharp ax. He saw the ax fall, and he shuddered.

Mortimer turned from side to side, mirroring the battle between the thoughts in his head. "The Queen was swift in her judgment." "But it was so brutal." "No, no, she was merciful to decree a quick death." "But the look on her face. She seemed to...enjoy it." "She is the Queen. No one questions her authority."

Mortimer closed his eyes tight and pulled a pillow over his head. He drifted off to sleep.

In his dream, Mortimer was on a ship sailing the ocean. He stood on the prow, gazing over the open sea, looking for a distant land. The wind whisped through his hair. The flag above him on the masthead rippled and furled as the ship crested, then dove into the waves.

Mortimer heard a deep laugh and turned to see Oberon standing on the deck. Mortimer's mother stood to Oberon's left. The door of the Captain's Galley opened and out stepped Eonder and Gwendolyn, who joined Oberon on deck. They all waved to Mortimer.

Mortimer woke up to the knock on his door. "Who is it?"

"It is Baldor, my lord. The Queen requests your presence for supper."

Mortimer did not answer. He looked at the golden helmet, the gift from Eonder, hanging from a brass hook on the wall. He clutched his backpack and opened the side flap and brought out the leather shield his mother had made for him. A tear formed in his eye. This was the shield that turned to shining silver and blinded Gharma when he and Eonder defeated the troll.

Eonder. Where was Eonder? Where was his mother, and Gwendolyn and Oberon? Mortimer put his face in his hands and sobbed.

Baldor continued knocking.

"My lord are you ill? May I help you?" Baldor's voice sounded frantic.

Mortimer wiped his nose and sniffled. He walked to the door and opened it.

Baldor stepped in and took one look at Mortimer. "I will tell the Queen that you are not well."

"No. That might make her angry. Tell her, tell her I need to wash up."

Baldor stepped back. "As you wish, my lord."

Mortimer was left alone in the room. He rinsed his face in the wash basin. Just then, he thought of the red apple from the garden. He lifted the side flap of his pack and grasped the apple from where he had left it. He pulled it out and held it far from his face.

The apple was no longer a delicious ruby color, but brown and bruised and misshapen. Mortimer remembered Eonder's words in the Willow Grove. "All things rot that stay long with the Queen." Mortimer opened his window and threw the apple as far as he could.

He shuffled down the hallway, then pulled back the double doors and stepped into the Banquet Room.

"Well, there is my little man. I thought you were going to miss supper. Come sit by me." Queen Valora sat upright and noble at the end of the table. "I have prepared a feast in your honor, for you are the one responsible for helping me retrieve my crown."

Mortimer gasped as he noticed the glorious golden crown that rested on Queen Valora's head. Her straight, black hair was a contrast to the luster and glory of the crown. Down the white skin of her neck hung a long silver chain with a green stone pendant resting on her chest. Her long, purple gown covered her wrists and ankles. Mortimer noticed tiny crescent moons and stars woven into the gown's fabric with golden thread.

"Where is your appetite? This is a celebration." The Queen said.

Mortimer looked at the empty chairs around the Banquet Table. "I...I do not feel well."

Queen Valora touched Mortimer's forehead.

"You poor dear. You are missing a delicious meal," she said as she took a bite of Cornish game hen.

Mortimer poked at the boysenberry torte on his plate. "How come there is nothing red in the castle?" he said.

Queen Valora choked. After wiping her mouth with a linen napkin, she said, "Why, you are a precocious boy. What a silly question. Whatever made you think of that?"

"Eonder told me to ask you." Queen Valora's face turned more pale than the white skin of her neck.

"Eonder? When did you see Eonder?"

Mortimer stabbed a boysenberry with his fork. "In the willow grove while Gharma was chanting to the moon."

The Queen's eyebrows raised and her lips pursed. She reached for the crown on her head as a slow smile spread across her ashen face.

She snapped her fingers. "More wine."

The attendant caught his foot on the corner of the Queen's chair. Dark wine spilled out of the silver pitcher he carried onto the white tablecloth and dripped down onto the floor.

"You imbecile," the Queen shouted as she whacked the attendant in the forearm with her scepter. "Clean this up." The frightened attendant bowed and backed away.

Mortimer watched the drops of wine on the white linen form a puddle. "It looks like blood," he said.

Queen Valora shrieked and bolted from her chair, knocking the crown from her head. "Do not ever mention that word."

Mortimer cowered. "What did I do?"

Queen Valora snarled and raised her scepter to strike. "You think you have beaten me? I have ascended the throne. I have the golden crown. I now rule the Western Lands."

Mortimer closed his eyes and lifted his arm to deflect the blow about to come.

"Get out." Her voice was shrill and cutting.

Mortimer pushed his chair away from the table and ran from the Banquet Room to his own room. He fell to his knees before the bed and sobbed for the second time that day.

Mortimer's Midnight Ride

Mortimer sat up and wiped his eyes. "I will not cry anymore. Not ever. Crying is for babies. Queen Valora would not cry." He tightened his jaw.

A flat piece of parchment slipped under the door. Mortimer retrieved it, but when he opened the door there was no one. Mortimer brought the parchment near the candlelight and read these words:

Mortimer,
Your life is in danger. You must escape!
Be ready at midnight.
Friends of the King

Mortimer wondered about the letter. Who wrote it? How did they know he was in danger? And why? He thought about marching right down the hallway to Queen Valora's room and showing her the letter. If it was true that he was in danger, then she, above all others, could protect him. Then Mortimer remembered the scene at dinner over the spilled wine and decided that disturbing the Queen was not a good idea.

Mortimer would have to solve this mystery on his own. Maybe he would uncover a plot against the Queen. He could expose the traitor and prove his worth. She would be happy again and make him her prince.

Mortimer filled his head with these thoughts as he stared into the flicker of the candle. His eyes closed.

Mortimer did not hear the key in his door nor hear a person enter. He awoke with the shaking of his shoulder. He rubbed his eyes and blinked before he recognized the person standing over him.

"Baldor?"

"You must leave. Now."

Mortimer tried to clear the cobwebs of sleep from his brain. "You sent the letter?"

"You are in grave danger. Here, change into these clothes." Baldor handed Mortimer a pair of woolen trousers and a tunic.

Mortimer took off the navy velvet ambassador's cap and started to unbutton his shirt. "What am I doing? What is this all about?"

"There is no time."

Mortimer folded his arms across his puffed out chest. "I order you to tell me, or I will go the Queen."

Baldor's face turned white. "She is the one you should fear."

"I do not believe you. She loves me."

"She loves only herself."

"I have a mind to report you to the Queen."

"Then both of us will be dead."

The conviction in Baldor's voice caught Mortimer off guard. "How do you know these things?"

"When you left the dinner table tonight, Valora continued to rant. She threw goblets and silverware across the room and ordered all of us out. I heard her screaming, "The blood did not defeat me. I killed him once, I can kill him again.""

"But what has that to do with me?"

"Did you not see the rage in her eyes when you mentioned the blood? You remind her of a past defeat and she will not allow that."

"I still do not understand."

Baldor looked over his shoulder as if the walls could hear. "The Book of the Ancients records that a King above all others laid down his life as a ransom for all. His sacrifice would make the way for his heir to bring peace throughout the land."

Mortimer sighed, "What do you want me to do?"

"I hid a rope under your bed if it was ever needed." Baldor reached under Mortimer's bed and secured one end of the rope to the bedpost while dropping the other out the window. "Someone, who is waiting for you down below, will take you to a safe location."

Mortimer felt the itchy wool of his pants and the coarse seams of his tunic. The clothes he had been wearing in the castle, the clothes of royalty, lay on his bed. "Are you sure about the Queen? I think she wanted to make me her prince."

Baldor stopped. "Did she tell you that?"

"Not exactly."

"She will share the throne with no one." Baldor handed the golden helmet to Mortimer. "Here, put this on."

"Why?"

"Two reasons, to protect your head as you climb down the rope, and to protect your mind from lies and deception."

Like a foggy dream, Mortimer remembered Eonder giving him the golden helmet. "All things rot that stay long with the Queen," he had once said. Mortimer stepped toward the window and peered down. He could not see the bottom through the thick fog and inky blackness of night. "I do not think I can do this."

Baldor handed Mortimer's backpack to him and his pointed stick. "If you stay, you will die."

Mortimer slipped the pack-straps over his shoulders and the stick into his belt-loop. He took one deep breath and lowered himself out the window. With his legs wrapped around the rope and his hands gripped tight, he inched his way downward.

Perspiration beaded on Mortimer's forehead, but he dared not loosen his hold to wipe it away. His heart pounded. It felt like he was descending into the Pit of Gwent where the wolves of Hades leapt to tear apart the souls that had dropped through the earth.

A firm hand gripped Mortimer's leg.

"I have you, now," said a deep voice through the fog.

Mortimer tried to scamper back up the rope, but a second hand reached up to pull him down.

Mortimer fell backward into strong arms.

"You are safe with me, little one."

Mortimer looked into the face of his protector. "Harlech. I am glad to see you."

Harlech lowered Mortimer's feet to the ground and tugged on the rope. The dim light in Mortimer's window was extinguished as the rope was pulled back in.

"Are you working for Baldor?"

Harlech grinned. "We are working together. We have both sworn an oath to protect you."

"Sworn an oath? To whom?"

"Why, King William, of course. Soon, you will meet him."

A peaceful, warm feeling filled Mortimer.

"We must go." Harlech lead Mortimer to two waiting horses. A mare whinnied. "It seems that Efleda missed you."

"Who?"

"Efleda, your horse. You mean to say you have forgotten her name?"

Mortimer hugged the mare's neck and whispered in her ear. "I am glad to see you again, Efleda." He hopped on her back. "Where are we going?"

"We will pass by the walls of the castle until we reach the path that leads to the Old Road. With God's help, the fog will give us cover." Mortimer, in his golden helmet, and

Harlech wearing the silver helm of the castle guard, could be spotted by reflected light if there were no fog.

Mortimer and Harlech passed below the east tower where a bonfire burned, providing warmth and light to the lonely soldiers relegated to night watch.

Harlech's horse stumbled, kicking pebbles on the path. He pulled the horse against the flat part of the wall.

"Halt! Who goes there." One of the soldiers waved a torch from the parapet. Mortimer and Harlech remained still. A few minutes after the torchlight disappeared, they ventured away from the wall and back onto the path.

Harlech veered due east and then north. Loose stones gave way to wet grass. Mortimer kept the tail of Harlech's horse in his sight. After going up and down many hills covered in dewy grass, Harlech stopped.

"I believe you know this place."

The fog had thinned and the clouds had parted, allowing pale moonlight to filter down. The castle was no longer in sight. In front of Mortimer was a stone wall as high as his knees.

"This is the garden that Gwendolyn and I discovered."

Harlech laughed. "You discovered? This garden has been here since the beginning of time."

"How do you know so much about it?"

"Let us say I know the Caretaker."

"What is the garden doing out here? And what purpose does the wall serve?"

Harlech laughed again. "You are inquisitive. Would you not agree that this is a perfect place for a garden? As for the wall, the purpose is to serve as a boundary."

"Ghimel said it was dangerous."

"Only to those whose hearts are full of evil."

Mortimer had many more questions but he thought it best to wait until the light of day. He yawned.

"Ah, yes, young one, it is quite late. A little while further and you shall have a soft bed and warm fire." Harlech turned and followed a cobblestone lane for a short distance before the lane disappeared beneath the grass.

They climbed more hills until a narrow path opened in a thicket of pine trees. Mortimer's mare stayed close behind Harlech. Mortimer's grip on the reigns loosened as his eyes tended to drift from open to shut and his head bobbed. Mortimer did not notice that Harlech had led them across a dirt road and into a thick grove of birch and elm trees.

Mortimer's head bobbed down again, then jerked upright when Efleda stopped.

Harlech lifted Mortimer from his horse. "Your journey has ended, little one."

Reunion

CHAPTER 15

Mortimer tried to open his groggy eyes. He could make out a light from a window in a stone cottage. Harlech helped him off his horse and through the door. Mortimer saw a cozy fire glowing in the hearth.

A man with a green cap sat with his back to the door. He knelt in front of the fireplace, stoking the logs into a flame. "Would you like to warm yourself beside the fire?" the man said.

"Yes, thank you, I would." Mortimer stepped closer to the fire, but to the left and behind the man.

"You are safe now, young one. I will feed and water the horses," Harlech said to Mortimer before he walked out the door.

Mortimer gave Harlech an apprehensive glance before he was left alone with the man with the green cap. Mortimer stood there rubbing his hands together for warmth.

"So you are on a journey. Travel far?" the man said.

"No. I do not think so. Just from the cas..." Mortimer bit his lip.

"You must be hungry from your ride. There is porridge in the pot and a bowl and spoon over there."

A clay bowl and wooden spoon lay on a table of dark wood. Light from the fire danced across strange letters carved into the border of the table. Mortimer brought the bowl and spoon to the copper kettle that hung from an iron rung built into the hearth.

Mortimer scooped up the porridge while trying to get a good look at the man.

The door opened, Harlech entered, blowing into his hands to warm them. "This is the coldest part of the night," he said.

"Come by the fire, my friend." The man stood to greet Harlech.

Harlech knelt before him. "My Lord."

Mortimer's mouth dropped open. It was then that he recognized Eonder's white flowing beard.

Eonder turned to Mortimer. "Do you know where you are?"

"Yes. In Gwendolyn's house."

"Do you know why you are here?"

Mortimer started to speak, then shook his head.

"Harlech has brought you to a safe place. Soon it will become apparent that your life is in danger. We must leave here before dawn."

Mortimer sat down at the table with his porridge and ran his fingers over the carved letters. Eonder and Harlech joined him. "What do these marks mean?"

"They tell of a king who ruled with power and justice."

"What happened to the king?"

"He died a noble death as a sacrifice for his people. He shed his blood that many might be saved. The runes you are feeling foretell of his coming again."

Mortimer looked around the room. It still smelled like cinnamon. "I wonder if..."

"If Gwendolyn is safe? Yes, she is. She and your mother are waiting for you on Oberon's ship."

Mortimer felt his throat tighten and his eyes water. He stiffened his back.

Eonder got up from the table. "I have some things already packed."

"How did you know that we would come here?"

Eonder smiled at Mortimer. "You are dear to my heart, young one. I have kept an eye out for you."

Mortimer felt his throat tighten again. He swallowed hard.

"And I am glad to see you wearing my present."

Mortimer felt the golden helmet on his head.

"Did she answer your question?"

Mortimer gave Eonder a puzzled look.

"The question of why she despises anything red."

Mortimer remembered the spilled wine at the dinner table and Queen Valora's explosive response. He shrugged his shoulders. "Something about blood."

"Do you still have the apple from my garden?"

"It turned brown. I threw it out." Mortimer felt uncomfortable, as if his soul was laid bare.

Eonder poured a bowl of water over the flame, causing the logs to sizzle. He checked for any glowing embers. "It is time to go."

"Why do we have to go now?"

"We are about to have an uninvited visitor. Valora has discovered that you are not in the castle, and has put a ransom for your head."

Mortimer felt a surge of defiance. "I do not believe you. She loves me."

Eonder sighed. "Ghimel thought she loved him, too. She promised him a throne next to her own. What was his fate?"

Mortimer shuddered. He could still see Ghimel blindfolded on the Block and the axe falling down. "He deserved to die."

"Did he? Are you a righteous judge? Can you see into the soul of a man?"

Mortimer folded his arms across his chest.

"Valora's words are enticing, and her beauty alluring, but death and destruction follow her like a moth to the flame."

Eonder snuffed out a lone candle. He, Mortimer and Harlech stepped outside the cabin. The first light of pink shone in the eastern sky.

"Come, I have a plan." Eonder opened the stable door. Efleda whinnied when she saw Mortimer.

"What is your bidding, my Lord?" Harlech said.

"Lead the horses on a diversion to the edge of the forest. Mortimer and I will meet you there."

"As you wish." Harlech grabbed the reigns of the other two horses and brought them out of the stable.

Before Mortimer could even ask why, Eonder turned to him. "Come, I want to show you something."

Mortimer followed Eonder up a ridge that looked down on Gwendolyn's house. They laid on soft pine needles to peer down on the path.

"Keep your helmet out of sight."

Mortimer unstrapped the golden helmet and poked his head up. There, on the path, coming towards Gwendolyn's house, was a shadow. Well, it seemed like a shadow, having a form that shifted, slithered and creeped.

"What is it?" Mortimer whispered.

"It is Eadwig, Valora's spy. He has followed you since The Lion's Paw."

"But why?"

"Word of your exploits have reached Valora. She sought to control you and the sword. Having failed, she seeks to kill you."

Eadwig crept to Gwendolyn's house. Without a sound, he sneaked around the front and peered into the window of the empty log cabin. He turned and lifted his head, sniffing the air.

He headed slowly up the hill where Mortimer and Eonder were hiding. Mortimer gasped. Underneath the hood of Eadwig's overcoat glowed yellow eyes. Eadwig reached into his coat and pulled out a dagger.

Mortimer felt the hairs stand up on the back of his neck. He grabbed the hilt of his sword, ready to brandish his powerful weapon.

A horse nickered far up the trail. Eadwig whirled toward the sound, then slunk down the hill and followed the trail.

Mortimer exhaled a deep breath.

"That has bought us some time. Come, we will catch up to Harlech and the horses."

Mortimer strapped on his helmet as he slid down the hill to follow Eonder.

The sky was lighter as Mortimer continued to follow Eonder up hills and down, over logs and through a brook. Mortimer reached into his pack for the compass Oberon had given him. They were headed west.

Then Eonder pulled back branches of a thick mulberry bush, allowing Mortimer to pass. There, not ten paces away, were Harlech and the horses.

"Did you see anyone?" Mortimer said to Harlech.

"Not with my eyes, but I felt a presence."

Mortimer looked over his shoulder. "Do you think he is still following?"

"Eadwig would have seen from the tracks that there was only one rider. He has returned to his master." Eonder mounted his horse. "We make for Helgath."

Noonday passed as they rode through a field of dandelions. The riders stopped for lunch near a stream, letting the horses water. An hour more of riding brought them to what seemed like an impenetrable wall of dried thickets.

Eonder dismounted and led the horses through. Mortimer felt a poke in his ribs and a tug on his sleeve as the branches jabbed at anything that moved. Soon, they were at the back wall to the city of Helgath.

As before, Eonder produced an iron key from his pocket. He pulled aside the wild vines to reveal the small arched door in the stone wall. The handle creaked, then turned.

They stayed on a narrow cobblestone lane that Mortimer and Eonder had traveled many days before. The horses neighed when they spotted Angwin's stable and their home. With a quick brush down, a meal of oats, and a hug for Efleda, Mortimer joined Eonder and Harlech up the alley to The Lion's Paw.

Eonder turned the latch on the back entrance door. The three entered what seemed like a deserted inn. There were no customers, no fire in the hearth, no aromas of things cooking in the kitchen.

"Angwin, are you anywhere about?" Eonder cupped his hands to his mouth to extend his voice.

There was a stirring in the back room. Ursula, Angwin's wife, entered through the kitchen. She did not lift her head, but mumbled, "Did you not see the sign?"

"We saw no sign. We came through the side entrance."

Ursula looked up when she recognized the voice. She dabbed at her red eyes. "Oh, Eonder, it is good to see you. Angwin will be sorry he missed you." Her lips quivered before the tears gushed. She wiped her eyes with her apron.

"Ursula, what happened here?" Eonder helped her to sit down.

"Lord Llandon came with soldiers the day you were here. They arrested my poor Angwin, then nailed a sign to the door that says, 'Off Limits'. What will happen to him?" She buried her face in her apron.

Eonder put his arm around her. "I shall return. And when I do, I will see that Llandon receives justice." He placed two gold coins on the table, then nodded toward the door.

Eonder, Mortimer and Harlech stepped into the side alley. "That man is beginning to make my blood boil." Eonder gripped his walking stick so tight that his knuckles turned white.

"What do we do now?"

"We make our way to Oberon's ship. Harlech, your castle guard uniform will make a perfect diversion. We will leave Helgath by the front gate."

The three merged into the chaos of vendors, merchants and buyers in the courtyard. Eonder tried to talk, but Mortimer could not hear him over the squawk of people. Eonder pointed to a hay wagon at the edge of the courtyard.

The driver of the wagon had his back turned as he leaned in close to a lady fruit vendor.

"Quick, climb under the hay." Eonder lifted Mortimer onto the backboard. "Harlech, when it is time, distract the guards at the gate and meet us at the dock."

Harlech nodded and ambled toward the iron gate of Helgath while Eonder hopped under the hay. The driver finished his flirting and climbed up into the seat of the wagon. The wagon lurched forward. Mortimer pulled the hay away from his face and peered out. Guards with pole axes were posted at the entrance and exit to Helgath.

As the hay wagon approached the gate, Mortimer sneezed.

"Eh, what's that? What you packing here?" the guard said to the driver.

"Hay. Hay for me horses, hay for me fields. You can keep anything else."

The guard stepped toward the driver. "Don't get lippy with me." The guard poked his pole axe into the hay piled in the wagon.

Just then Harlech walked up. The guard stood to attention. "Beggin' your pardon, captain."

"What is the problem here?" Harlech said to the driver.

"Ask 'im. He thinks I have critters in me hay."

Harlech poked into the hay with the flat of his sword. "It feels like hay to me. You can pass." The wagon continued through the stone tunnel and out the front gate.

When the cobblestone turned to dirt Eonder touched Mortimer's arm.

"Get ready to jump."

Mortimer crawled to the edge of the wagon and slid off the back and onto a dirt road.

The stone towers of Helgath were well behind them. The dirt road became sandy as Mortimer and Eonder approached the dock. They stood and waited for Harlech. Soon, his figure could be seen coming down the trail. A tall, striking man wearing the silver helm of the castle guard over shoulder mail and leather jerkin, a sword strapped to his side.

A few fishermen milling around the dock lifted a wary eye when they saw Harlech.

"What now?" Mortimer said.

"We wait. An opportunity will present itself." Eonder leaned on his walking stick.

"We best be shoving off if you want to be fishing."

Mortimer saw a man about sixty years old with hunched shoulders and a grizzled face standing there. His arms were wiry with strong hands.

"Kept the boat for ya over here. Still got time before the sun goes down." The man extended three fishing poles.

Eonder took one of the poles. "Sorry we are late. We were delayed."

The man guided them into a rowboat moored to the dock, untied the rope and pushed off. He looked up to the fishermen on the dock. "Gonna catch me some big ones this time." The fishermen laughed and waved.

Once the rowboat had cleared the breaking waves, the man extended his hand to Eonder. "Name's Ben."

"I am Eonder, and this is Harlech and Mortimer."

Ben nodded and resumed his rowing. "Oberon's ship is anchored back in a cove."

"You know Oberon?" Mortimer said.

"Met him a few days ago. Told me to keep an eye out for the comings and goings in the city."

Mortimer could contain his curiosity no longer. "How did you know it was us? I mean, you were looking for us?"

When Ben laughed, he revealed two missing front teeth. "Oberon said you'd be coming. I didn't plan on no soldier, though. That threw me for a second."

The rowboat cleared a rock outcropping and entered a shallow cove. There, with colored shields reflecting the afternoon sunlight, was The Morning Star.

A lookout onboard yelled, "Oh hoy," and lowered a rope ladder over the hull. Ben tied off his rowboat and all four climbed aboard the ship.

Mortimer saw his mother standing on the deck and ran to hug her. Gwendolyn ran past him to hug her grandfather. Marallon brushed the hair out of Mortimer's eyes and kissed him on the forehead.

"Thank God you are here," she said.

Oberon, who had been standing next to Marallon, reached over with one arm wrapped around Mortimer's shoulder. The squeeze lifted Mortimer off the deck. "Good to see you, lad."

Mortimer relaxed in Oberon's strength. When Oberon let go, Gwendolyn was waiting for him.

"I knew you would come, I just knew it." She hugged him.

Mortimer blushed.

"A fair wind blows. Where do we sail, my Lord?" Oberon said to Eonder.

"Yes, the winds are changing. We sail North to Barwick's Bay. It is time to gather the Council." Eonder turned to Ben. "Would you sail with us? I would very much like to hear of what you have seen at Helgath."

Ben's face lit up. "I have dreamed of riding the waves in a vessel so fine."

Oberon nodded. "Hoist the anchor and lower the sail. Make way for Barwick's Bay."

A warm wind caught the sails, propelling The Morning Star into the open seas. The sun sank into the farthest reaches of the ocean, causing the sky to ripple flaming red.

Gwendolyn grabbed Mortimer's hand. "I want to hear all about what happened to you in the castle."

Mortimer lowered his head and mumbled.

"This is a cause for a celebration," Oberon said. "Have the cook prepare a feast."

Mortimer looked across the foaming waves to where the White Castle would be.

Eonder put his arm around Mortimer. "You are with the ones who love you the most. This is where you belong."

Mortimer looked up to see the first star of the night flicker in the sky. He closed his eyes and made a wish, then walked below with Eonder to join the others for a celebration supper.

Thus ends the second book of the Mortimer Trilogy. The third book, The King Revealed, tells the tale of Mortimer's escape from assassins, the allegiance of his soul, and the epic battle that will determine the fate of the kingdom.

This is the conclusion of the second book of the Adventures of Mortimer trilogy. The third story, The King Revealed, describes Mortimer's quest for his father and purpose in life, set around the epic battle for control of the kingdom.